# WHO SAYS THAT?

• WORDS BY Arnold L. Shapiro

• PICTURES BY Monica Wellington

shhh

shhh
shhh

Dutton Children's Books • New York

# Monkeys chatter.

# Cats purr.

purr purr

purrrrrrrrrr

purr

purr
purr
purr

purr
purr
purr

Lions roar.

ROAR

# Hummingbirds whir.

# Squirrels chitter.

chitter
chitter
chitter

chitter
chitter
chitter

# Cows moo.

# Bears growl.

Owls whoo.

But

# girls and boys make different noise!

whisper

giggle
giggle
giggle

# Mice squeak.

# Parrots shriek.

# Snakes hiss.

# Beavers smack.

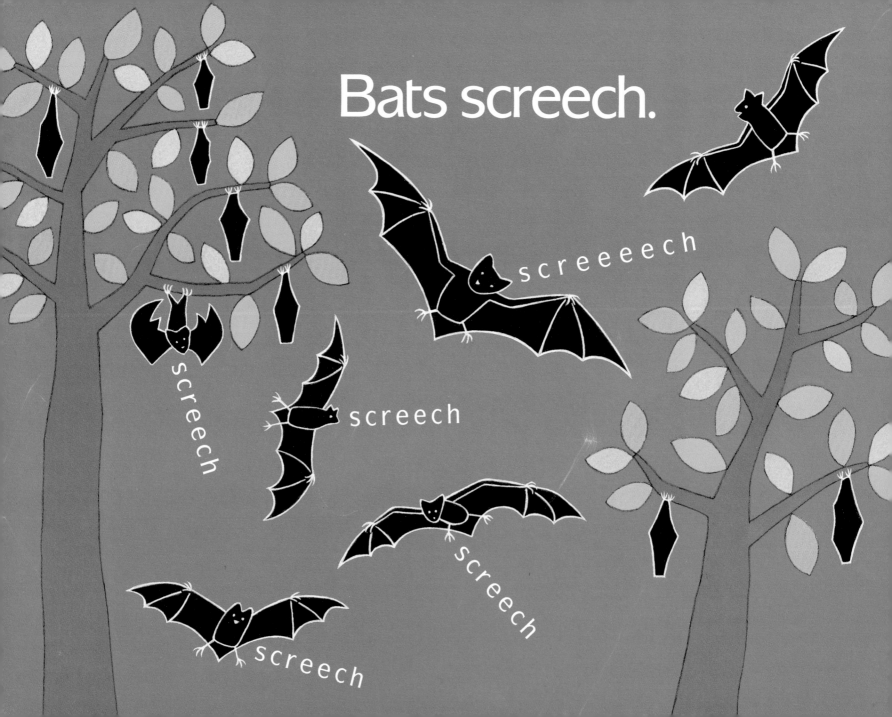

Bats screech.

screeeech

screech

screech

screech

screech

# Ducks quack.

But

# girls and boys make different noise!

SHOUT SHOUT SHOUT SHOUT

sing sing sing

chuckle

talk

# Flies hum.

# Robins cheep.

# Seals bark.

# Chicks peep.

# Sheep baa.

baaaaa

baaaa

baa

baaaa

baaaa

baaaa

Bees buzz.

# Ponies neigh.

But

YELL

whistle whistle

# girls and boys make different noise!

holler

holler

holler

SCREAM

SCREAM

SCREAM

snicker

snicker

laugh

laugh

baa bay buzz neigh chatter purr roar whir chitter moo growl whoo oink squeak chirp shriek hiss smack screech quack hum cheep bark peep

To Deborah,
Danny, Kenny, and Michael, my girl and boys.
May you always make a different noise. • A.L.S.

for Lydia • M.W.

Library of Congress Cataloging-in-Publication Data
Shapiro, Arnold, date.
Who says that? / words by Arnold L. Shapiro; pictures by Monica Wellington.—1st ed.
p. cm.
Summary: Rhyming text enumerates the many different sounds made by animals,
from the chatter of monkeys to the neighing of ponies.
ISBN 0-525-44698-2
[1. Animal sounds—Fiction. 2. Stories in rhyme.] I. Wellington, Monica, ill. II. Title.
PZ8.3.S5294WK 1991 [E]—dc20 90-3996 CIP AC

Published in the United States by Dutton Children's Books,
a division of Penguin Books USA Inc.

Designer: Alice Lee Groton

Printed in Hong Kong by South China Printing Co.
First Edition 10 9 8 7 6 5 4 3 2 1